Valentine's Day

Story by Carole Mohr
Illustrations by Mark Weber

Dr. Judith Nadell, Series Editor

"Today is Valentine's Day," said Mrs. Hall.

"Let's make Valentine cards!"

"Yay!" shouted the class.

Uu Vv Ww Xx Yy Zz
Mrs Hall

"Here are red paper and white paper.
Use them to make your Valentine card."

Your card could say...
I like you.
or
I love you.
or
You are the best.
or
You are special.
Mrs. Hall
1

"Here are glue sticks, markers, and scissors. Use them to make your Valentine card."

Glue Sticks

Derek cut out a big red heart.

He put it on white paper.

Kendra cut out a big white heart.

She put it on red paper.

Victor cut out little red hearts.

He put them on white paper.

Jasmin cut out little white hearts.

She put them on red paper.

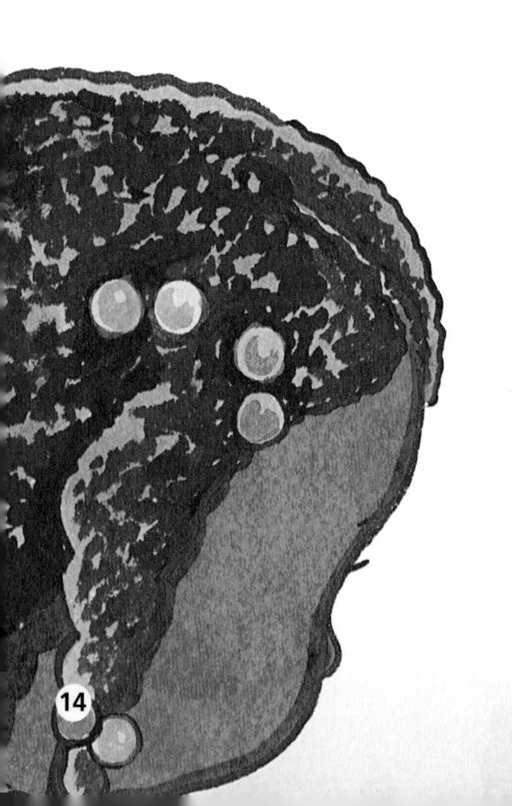

"May I see your Valentine cards?"
said Mrs. Hall.

"Surprise!" shouted the class.
"Our cards are for you!"